High School Stories

Short Takes from the Writers' Club

Mary M. Nyman

iUniverse, Inc.
New York   Bloomington

High School Stories
Short Takes from the Writers' Club

iUniverse books may be ordered through booksellers or by contacting:

iUniverse
1663 Liberty Drive
Bloomington, IN 47403
www.iuniverse.com
1-800-Authors (1-800-288-4677)

ISBN: 978-1-4502-1585-5 (sc)
ISBN: 978-1-4502-1586-2 (ebk)

Printed in the United States of America

iUniverse rev. date: 3/24/2010

For my children and grandchildren

Contents

Author's Notes and Acknowledgments

High School Stories grew out of many years of teaching high school English and raising five wonderful children. I am very grateful for these experiences, and I would like to share my impressions with teenagers today, because young people continue to inspire me. Perhaps parents and teachers will relate to some of these stories as well, since what happens here is universal.

I am very much indebted to my friend, Carol Rossi, for her patience and assistance in preparing this manuscript; and I especially want to thank my instructor, author, and editor, Steven Manchester, for his invaluable help and expertise with revising and formatting. Finally, I want to thank my daughter, Helen, for helping me with the technology involved in submitting this manuscript and for her final editing and suggestions pertaining to characterization.

Introduction

(The Writers' Club)

High school was never easy. There was always something unpleasant to face, a lot of it academic. I remember well the boredom and horrors of calculus and chemistry, the never-ending pressures of homework deadlines, and my mother's frequent nagging—not to mention having to participate in gym when I was too tired to get out of bed in the morning. It was pretty hard to avoid things I didn't like, and it was pretty hard to get away with things I thought I would like. Thinking back, it seemed like someone was always watching out for me, which I, of course, didn't appreciate at the time.

Not that I would like to relive these four years, because we also had to face the deeper problems of growing up. We had to find ourselves, which we know now is a lifelong process. And we had to learn how to be ourselves.

It has been two years since the events of my junior year took place. You may remember, I told the story about that year (and the near disasters I experienced) in a book called *When the Leaves Fall*. It's a book about how I survived drug abuse by making decisions that saved my life. Well, I've just finished my freshman year in college, taking courses and working; and my close friend, Stephanie, is also in college. I am Corey, in case you haven't read my book.

All in all life is pretty good right now, especially since I have Stephanie, who just might become the real love of my life when we're ready. But nobody gets out of high school without having to face some tough times. And Stephanie had the brilliant idea of hosting a writers' club as a good way to keep in touch with our high school friends. This meant that we would meet once every two months and share ideas for stories about memorable events that had happened to us over the past six years. After that, the assignment would be to write a good short story to read to the other members of the group.

Most of my friends have had to face some pretty difficult issues. In *High School Stories* you can experience their feelings about bullying and the deaths of favorite grandparents, about having to enable and take care of messed up parents, and about acknowledging mixed feelings toward popular kids. They also tell about dealing with unwanted pregnancy and homosexuality, the death of friendship or friends, and drug abuse and its consequences. If you've had to face any of these situations, perhaps you'll be able to relate to these stories. You'll discover how my friends handled their problems, and maybe their insights can help provide you with some answers. At the very least, I hope you'll realize that you are not alone.

Well, the time has come for our group to meet and share their stories. We figured that we could read all of them in one evening, so we met at Stephanie's house for pizza, and, afterward, here's what we shared.

Sarah's

Sarah's Day Off

Sarah was fifteen years old and five foot five. She considered herself an all-around average girl, and she loved being a babysitter at the ski lodge in central Maine. Her smile was warm and engaging, and she was open, friendly, and at times even childlike. Her caring attitude made her a favorite among the vacationing families.

To those around her, she seemed so happy and serene, but appearances can be misleading. No one could have known what she was feeling inside.

As she looked out on the white mountainous world surrounding the lodge, she watched the skiers making their way through the snow. Their rosy faces showed the undeniable happiness that comes from being on vacation, protected from the nagging everyday routines by the magnificence of this place. Sarah understood, and she felt envious.

Tired and ready for the day to be done, she looked at her watch again. It was time for the ski lifts to shut down. Soon the tired and happy skiers would be crowding the entrance to the lodge. As snow began to fall on the world outside the window, Sarah foresaw her own time in her own private world, out there, away from the vacationers and the slopes—time away from everything so she could think.

In spite of her feelings of relative calm now, yesterday's events suddenly resurfaced, bringing with them a familiar feeling of anxiety. As she stood, rearranging her favorite teddy bears and books on the playroom shelves, she found herself close to tears. *I'm just overtired, or maybe I'm hungry*, she thought as she watched the orange sun dipping

1

slowly behind the mountains, pulling its glistening golden ribbons up over the darkening slopes. Sunsets had always been spectacular here, but today she was just too numb to be affected. *For an artist, that's not so good,* she reflected.

She found her coat and rummaged through the junk in her pocket for a Heath bar. She was so bone tired that she felt unrelated to all her body parts. Her slim feet seemed miles away, and the mirror in the corner of the nursery revealed a slight puffiness under her eyes. *Not bad,* she thought, *considering my frame of mind. But those bangs sure need trimming.* She pushed a few stray strands of hair back from her face and then surveyed the rest of her trim, compact figure, wondering somberly what she would look like by the time she reached her next birthday.

The door of the ski lodge burst open, and a throng of rowdy skiers filled the entryway. In the middle, head and shoulders above the rest, stood her idol, Charlie. He was always there. In fact, when she was little, he had taught her how to ski. He was so handsome and charming that all the girls fell in love with him. As usual, he had a girl on each arm and he was talking and laughing boisterously. *How could I have fallen for someone so fickle?* Sarah was thinking.

She winced and quickly stepped back into the nursery, hoping he hadn't seen her. Suddenly, she felt very small and alone. *What's the use in hiding?* she reflected. *Most of the time he doesn't even acknowledge my presence anyway. Just like the way he snubbed me yesterday.*

But she was too late. His hearty voice boomed out across the room. "Sarah!"

"Hi, Charlie." As he drew attention to her, she was sure she saw him wink at one of the other girls.

"Skiing was beautiful. Too bad you couldn't join us on the slopes today."

"Was it?" she answered weakly, trying to keep her voice cool and impersonal.

"Yeah, sure." Then he added, "At least you can join us for hot chocolate before they close the snack bar."

The question in his voice hung enticingly over her head. *But he doesn't know about us, does he? I bet he'd change his tune in a heartbeat if he knew about our little predicament,* a nagging voice reminded her.

"Thanks anyway, but my mom will be picking me up any minute."

"Okay. See you soon?"

Maybe. But why never at night or on a date anymore? Resentment welled up inside her so suddenly that it surprised her. She'd thought she was over him.

Charlie always radiated an almost godlike presence. His exuberance overwhelmed her. And, like everyone else, she had been mesmerized by his magnetism. But the spell didn't last. Now she was feeling more isolated and insignificant than ever. *Why couldn't I see through him before? And why do I still feel this way about him now?* Her ambivalence confused her.

She was feeling that empty feeling she always got when she wasn't communicating with Charlie. She'd have to take a backseat, so to speak, to the new girls in his life. Now she would have to go home and face Sunday, schoolwork, and a long stretch of time alone with her thoughts. Suddenly she saw herself at the end of a long, dark tunnel that emptied into bright nothingness—into a nagging problem she didn't want and didn't know how to share with anyone

The sound of snow crunching under tires and then the honk of a horn told Sarah her mother had arrived. Wearily, she picked up her coat and hat and hurried out of the lodge. The front seat of her mom's old Honda was piled high with laundry. Sarah groaned, pushed the seat forward, and climbed into the back where their dog, Blackie, greeted her with his usual friendly bark.

It was a relief to be going home after such a long day of minding the skiers' children. *Come to think of it, today is March 18. After next weekend the ski lodge will be closed for the season,* Sarah thought as she snuggled into the warmth of the moving car. *What if this turns out to be my last season at the lodge?*

Don't think about that now, Sarah. For now, just look forward to the rest of the weekend.

They rode in silence along the sparkling road. The stars were already bright in the darkening sky and the icy surface of the lake glittered softly. *How beautiful it is to live here,* Sarah thought, *among the lakes and pine forests and happy vacationers.* Suddenly, she felt close to tears.

Beauty often made her cry. But she knew that wasn't the reason she felt like crying.

She was looking out the window at the contrast of the snow against the darkness. *It's like my big problem,* she thought. *Lies against the truth, or something like that.*

"Mom? Why are we taking this road? The other is faster, and I'm so tired."

"I know you're tired, dear, but I need to stop at the grocery for a few things."

"Oh, Mom, can't it wait until tomorrow?"

"No. We need milk and eggs for breakfast, and you know it's miles to the store. It's enough to drive twenty miles to the lodge, especially when the roads are so icy."

Sarah felt a twinge of guilt, and her head was beginning to ache. "But, Mom, it's so cramped in here, and I can't get comfortable. Blackie, stop crowding me!"

"What's with you, Sarah? He's just trying to be friendly. Why are you complaining so much? It's just not like you. You aren't yourself lately. Are you sick? Or just grumpy?"

Sarah was quiet. *Oh, Mom, I don't want to shut you out, and I so need to talk to you, now. But how? The burden of keeping this secret is getting too heavy. I can hardly bear it. But what else can I do? Oh, if I could just be your little girl again and crawl up on your lap and into your arms. You would comfort me so much. If only I knew how to share my problem with you.*

She turned to her mother and opened her mouth to say something, but nothing particularly meaningful came out. "I'm okay, Mom. I'm just overtired, that's all." She clamped her mouth shut, turned away, and pretended to focus on the passing scenery.

But her thoughts were going around in circles. How would she ever be able to face the unpleasantness and disappointment she would see in the faces of her mother and stepfather if she told them the truth? Thinking of the disruption she would be causing in everyone's life was almost more than she could bear. There would be no going back after everything was out in the open.

"Maybe if you tried to sleep for awhile, the time would pass faster," her mother suggested.

Yeah. As if I want time to pass faster. Just let me disappear for a long time.

But the warmth of the car and the hum of the engine must have lulled her to sleep because suddenly they were home. The rambling farmhouse, with its long front porch and familiar rounded columns, loomed before her like a great white fortress. *Maybe it will swallow me up and protect me,* she told herself, smiling at the picture painted before her. *Maybe the problem will just ... go away.*

The car stopped and Sarah, renewed by her brief nap, jumped out and raced up the steps. She threw open the door, ran down the hall, and flung her coat on the bench before bursting into the warm glow of the bright yellow kitchen.

Almost too quickly, she came to a halt. The smell of roasted chicken and baked potatoes, her favorites, brought the now familiar feeling of nausea. *Oh,* she thought, repressing the urge to be sick, *I almost forgot. Why must I keep remembering?* Quickly she checked herself. *Just try to act natural, Sarah. They mustn't know.*

Trying to appear calm and hungry, she excused herself and went upstairs. Soon, she heard her mother's voice. "Sarah, please wash up. Dinner's ready."

Sarah spent a long time washing. As she let the warm water run over her cold hands, she stared at her reflection in the mirror. *Just get through dinner,* she coached herself. *Go downstairs and join your parents and do your best to eat a reasonable amount. And try to be pleasant.* She practiced a smile and then headed downstairs, hoping that maybe, if she was quiet, her parents just wouldn't pay attention to her.

For the most part it seemed to work. During dinner she thought she saw her mother and stepfather exchanging glances, but all her mother said was, "Sarah, dear, are you feeling all right?"

Sarah nodded. "I'm just tired, that's all."

Dinner seemed to last a very long time. *I have to get out of here.* She yawned and then politely asked if she could be excused from dessert, stating that she needed to get started reading the book for her report.

"My, aren't we the studious one!" exclaimed her stepfather as she rose to leave the table.

Sarah let the comment pass and hurried out of the room. *If only he knew.* She shuddered as she climbed the stairs to her bedroom. She turned on the radio and flopped down on her soft bed, hugging her large bolster pillow and trying to keep from crying. She yawned again. She was so tired.

Suddenly she found herself outside of the house again. It was snowing, and the frigid wind bit her skin. *Why don't I have a coat on?* She ran up to the front door, but it was locked and she couldn't get in. Frantic, she pounded and pounded, but no one came. She looked around her. It was very dark, and the car was gone. The only light she could see was coming from her own bedroom window. It cast a strange glow out over the thin coat of snow. Everything was eerie and, except for the slight crackling of frozen branches, terribly quiet.

As time seemed to cease, Sarah stood there, shivering. She strained forward, listening for some familiar sound. But there was nothing. Nothing at all. Suddenly she could bear it no longer. She yelled out, "Is anyone home?" and then, with tears of frustration, "Where is everybody? Where have you all gone?" There was no answer.

She saw that the barn door was ajar and she called out to Blackie. He was always on guard, but where was he tonight? At last, without warning, the horror of her situation dawned on her. *They've gone away and left me out in the cold all alone. What will I do? Where will I go?*

The scene whirled around her. She backed across the front porch and down the steps. She looked up at her window and then she froze in terror. What she saw was a familiar shadow in front of the light, and the shadow was moving. Suddenly a gust of wind blew the window open. Sarah covered her mouth to stop her screams. She saw herself standing in her room holding the baby in her arms. Then, she heard her double let out a piercing and terrible laugh.

Sarah awoke in a cold sweat. She had no covers over her, and her teeth were chattering. Her feet dangled over the edge of her bed, her arm was asleep, and her neck hurt from being turned to the side on her bolster pillow. She was completely exhausted. All she wanted to do was sleep and forget.

Weakly, she slipped off her shoes, pulled down the covers, and got back into bed, clothes and all. She pulled the blankets over her head and turned out the light. *I have to learn to face the dark,* she thought. *And these nightmares . I've got to do something to make them go away.* She lay awake thinking long into the night.

The next morning Sarah woke up to a blue sky and her day off. It was Sunday, and she knew what she would have to do. There was no longer any question about it. She climbed out of bed and out of yesterday's clothes. She dressed carefully, reflecting upon the decision that she had just made and the feeling of well-being it brought. She went downstairs and found her mother, alone in the kitchen, preparing breakfast.

"Mom," she said, "I have something I need to talk to you about."

Cindy's

Maybe Next Fall

It was one of those spectacular evenings in mid-May when the fragrance of the white lilacs hung heavy in the air. The moon was a great golden promise in the sky, its shimmering reflection weaving a magical path across the lake. It was a night for dreamers.

Cindy felt the beauty of it all as she sat curled up on the window seat in the quiet study room of her dormitory. The breeze touched her face as she lingered in her reverie, unwilling to break the spell this change of seasons had cast over her.

Suddenly, the silence was shattered. Breathless from climbing the flight of stairs, Janet burst into the room. "Cindy, there's a phone call for you."

Cindy looked at her watch, and a premonition cut through her like a sharp knife. No one ever called her after ten o'clock at night. She knew immediately that something awful had happened. She ran for the stairs, with Janet at her heels. When they reached the phone, she grabbed her friend's hand. "Janet, stay with me," she pleaded.

The receiver felt cold and there was static on the line.

"Cindy? Cindy, is that you?" She could hear the old, familiar tension in her mother's voice.

Her mother, the weak and controlling victim. What had she gotten herself into now?

Cindy forced herself to sound pleasant, but even to her it seemed unnatural. "Hi, Mom. How are things? What's happened? Why are you calling me so late?"

"Cindy, I need you to come home right away."

Inwardly, Cindy groaned. "You mean leave college?"

"Yes, honey. Your stepfather is in the hospital. He collapsed at work today."

"Oh, no. I am really sorry to hear that, Mom."

"You know I'm due next week, and now this."

Cindy could just picture her mother wringing her hands.

"Well, you know I have exams next week. I've been doing so well and studying so hard to get ready. These exams are so important, and—"

"Well, you can make up your exams later. I need you home right now."

"But, Mom!"

"You need to leave right away—tonight—and come home," her mom repeated. "We all need you so badly, honey."

Cindy felt a familiar wave of guilt wash over her, and all the conflicts surfaced again. *Am I being selfish? Is it wrong to be angry when I feel so trapped?*

"Sure, Mom. Of course I'll be there. See you soon."

Cindy replaced the phone and leaned against the wall, shaking uncontrollably. Janet caught her arm. "What is it?"

Cindy didn't answer.

"Come on. Let's go to our room," Janet said.

Cindy followed in stunned silence. She sat down on her bed. As she considered the situation, the tears came, and so did the questions. *What do I do now? Those exams are important, and I've been doing so well. How can my parents do this to me? How can my stepfather do this to me? He is supposed to take care of my mother.*

In thinking back she remembered what a nightmare her senior year in high school had been. She was in continual turmoil, always reacting to the latest crisis in her parents' lives. But now, being away at college, she finally felt centered. The past nine months had been a struggle, but Greenbriar had helped her break loose from the responsibility she had felt for her mother's depression after the divorce and remarriage.

It had taken a whole semester for Cindy to do that and to bring her marks up. Now she was being asked to assume responsibility again, and not only for her mother this time, but for her stepfather as well. And to top it off, her mother, at age forty-seven, was about to have twins. This was like adding insult to injury. It was so embarrassing.

Cindy felt trapped. It just wasn't fair. Her tears of frustration reminded her of the resentment she felt toward her family. She knew she had a right to feel as she did. And there was another problem that she just couldn't ignore, and that was Todd—wonderful, understanding Todd. They'd been going together for almost three months, and now she was being asked to give him up, too. *Parents! Why can't they take care of the messes they get themselves into?* she wondered.

Janet sat down next to her. "Do you want to talk about it?"

"I have to leave. My stepfather is very ill."

"Oh, no! What about finals?"

Cindy shrugged weakly.

"I'll help you pack."

Together, they dragged an ancient suitcase out from under the bed and began piling clothing, books, and papers into it. Next, they stuffed two duffel bags with bedding and coats, and a laundry bag with shoes and boots. Then Cindy headed for her cubby in the bathroom, where her toiletries were kept. Janet helped tighten the caps on her makeup jars, so they wouldn't spill in her dressing case.

Finally, everything was packed—books, papers, clothes and all— just in case she couldn't get back. At that moment she was struck by the realization that she might not return. Good things in her life always seemed to come to an end. Suddenly, it all closed in on her. "Oh, Janet. Why did this have to happen now? What am I going to do? I know I won't get back. The time is too short. How will I take my finals? What will I do without Todd? We have been so happy together. Will my teachers understand? Could you talk to them tomorrow?"

"Consider it done. Right now, though, I'll call the bus station. And do you want me to call Todd?"

"No, I'll call him."

Todd arrived at 11:30, looking serious and concerned. He had called a taxi, and it was waiting to take them to the bus station four miles away. The bus would be arriving at midnight. *The witching hour*, Cindy thought grimly. *Only thirty minutes to the end of a beautiful relationship.* She felt the tears of anger and frustration welling up again. *I'll have to control myself. I don't want Todd to know how I really feel. He wouldn't respect me if he knew I wanted to dump my whole family.*

"Let's hope the bus driver will let you on without a ticket at this hour," Todd said, squeezing her arm gently.

Cindy smiled, noting his caring and warm appraisal of her. She had thrown on her hot pink sweater and jeans, along with the crazy pink sneakers Todd liked. *At least I can pretend to see the bright side of things and hope for that magic path to the moon.* For a moment the image reappeared, and its beauty and serenity overwhelmed her.

She knew she had to appear calm. Todd liked girls who didn't let their emotions get the better of them. He also liked blondes. She hoped her hair would be blonder after the summer. But a distressing thought occurred to her. *What if I can't come back? Will he find another blonde to replace me?*

The cab was idling outside the dorm. Todd piled her luggage on the floor in the back and got in with her. He put his arm around her while he gave directions to the driver. Then, too quickly, the depot loomed in front of them. *I don't want to cry,* she thought, *and I won't.* She forced back her feelings as the taxi driver dragged her heavy luggage from the cab.

She stood with Todd on the platform, and he took her hands in his. She sensed he understood her tightly controlled feelings and her inability to say anything.

"I hate to see you go, Cindy. I'll miss you a lot."

She nodded. She was so miserable. And then the words just tumbled out. She couldn't stop them. "I hate having to take care of my parents. When I left home, I thought I'd be able to take care of me, for a change. And what about us?"

He took her in his arms. "Dear Cindy. You don't have to take care of me. I'm not like your parents." Then he stepped back and lifted her chin with his finger. "You know, I lost my father a year ago."

This was something he had never discussed with her before. "I know it's tough, but you know you won't forgive yourself if you aren't there for your family right now. There will be plenty of time later for us to enjoy being together."

Cindy was so overcome that she didn't know how to answer. She thought, *Just saying "good-bye" is inappropriate, and "I'm sorry" isn't enough.*

But Todd was strong. *Maybe ... just maybe.*

Todd took her face between his hands and kissed her gently. "You know I love you," he said. "We'll see each other again. Maybe when the colors of autumn show their most brilliant."

Cindy boarded the bus, holding back tears. She managed a brief smile, but inside, she was really hurting. She knew she needed to keep herself together, to stay strong for what she would have to face at home, but it was all so scary and sad. What if she never saw Todd again?

She couldn't bear to think of that now. Instead she closed her eyes and focused on Todd's words, holding them in her heart as tightly as she could. *"Maybe, when the colors of autumn show their most brilliant."* *Maybe—just maybe—.*

Tim's

Student of the Month

"Worthington. What a name for this unworthy town!" Tim exclaimed. He slid past his homeroom teacher and into his desk at the sound of the late bell. *I know they'll announce it today and I know I've lost the bet. Missy always knows how they'll vote,* he reminded himself.

"A moment of silence," commanded the voice on the intercom. After this joke called silent prayer, there followed a list of guidance passes, yesterday's sports victories, and then the house-of-correction scenario, something about graffiti on the restroom walls. *This is the dead of winter, when everybody is depressed and bored,* Tim thought, *and this negative stuff just makes it worse.* He stretched out, changing his position, as his legs felt cramped under the small desk.

"And now for the announcement you've all been waiting for," the voice continued. "The student of the month at Worthington High is none other than John Mathias!"

Tim was really annoyed, though he tried to appear unfazed. He wondered if the others sensed his feelings of disgust. *But then, isn't this outcome predictable? Since when does a person's values or superior grades triumph over being a successful athlete?* Tim watched as his classmates congratulated their number one football and basketball hero. Amid the stamping feet and cheering voices sat John, smiling his smug, self-confident smile.

Well, an academic genius doesn't make it, as usual. Five dollars down the drain again, Tim was thinking. He was resigned to defeat.

As the voice continued with the announcements, the room gradually quieted. "Thanks to your school committee's recent vote, vacation will start early, at eleven o'clock on Friday. Now our athletes can rest up for the big game Friday night."

The bell rang. Tim watched as the team carried John down the hall. *An awesome day for some of us,* he thought. *I wonder how Missy feels, the way he's been treating her lately.* He started down the hall toward his locker.

"Oh no, late again," he muttered as he fumbled with his combination. "Now, where's that law book?"

Then he saw her. Missy was standing in front of her locker, unbuttoning her coat. It was really unlike her to be late. Then Tim realized she'd been crying. He walked over, wanting to ask is she was okay; but instead, he quietly took her books and they started down the hall together. At the classroom door, he handed them back, and she wiped her eyes and smiled.

God, she's beautiful! But she doesn't want to connect us. He could understand that, for now anyway. She was the number one scholar in her class, with straight A plus marks in academics and citizenship and good at everything except athletics. *But she's sure hurting today.* It saddened him to think about it because he realized he really couldn't do anything about it. She wasn't his girlfriend, even though he was imagining what it might be like if this happened.

Finally they were seated, and Mr. Corriveau took attendance. The students were still rowdy and excited, all except Tim and Missy. She kept looking at John who was ignoring her and leaning in close to talk to Tracey.

If he gets any closer, he'll be sitting in her lap. Everybody knows what she's like, but nobody ever says anything. But hey, what do you expect? Her father is third generation, from an established family, president of the bank, and chairman of the town's selectmen. So who's going to admit that his daughter's the fastest girl in town, and an addict, too?

I'd sure like to have my own Porsche and spending money. It's pretty obvious what John wants from her, even though he's been going out with Missy. He wants to have it all but he doesn't even know what he's got. Tracey's cheap. John gets what he wants when he wants it. Why doesn't that guy wise up? All this rah-rah for his friends and "yes, sir, no, sir" for the teachers—. *Well, as they always say, "pride comes before a fall." Maybe he's an athlete who'll die young. I couldn't care less if it weren't for Missy.*

He saw Missy turn away, trying not to acknowledge John's obvious play for Tracey. Tim sympathized. He understood what it meant not to be the most popular, most sought-after person in school. Grades obviously weren't the most important thing at Worthington High. *I could improve my grades, though, and I could admit to what I see, but what's the use? The jocks always win around here.*

All through the class period, Tim couldn't stop looking at Missy. She appeared to be listening to every word, taking notes as she always did, but he knew she was hurting inside. *Why doesn't she stand up to him?* Tim asked himself. *In some ways she's like John. She likes being first and she's willing to risk being hurt in order to date a class hero.*

When the bell rang, Missy quickly left the room and started down the hall. Tim followed at a distance, not wanting to intrude on her private thoughts. John had left with Tracey and the others, and he hadn't even acknowledged Missy's presence. *Boy, that's cold,* Tim thought. *Success sure has gone to that guy's head.*

Now he was angry. *Someone ought to talk to that girl. She's got so much going for her. Why does she hang around with such a two-faced creep?*

Tim continued down the hall but stopped when he reached the corner. There was John, forcefully taking Missy's arm and guiding her toward the gym. Tim hung back, but he couldn't help overhearing.

"Hey, why aren't you congratulating me like the others? Don't you care? I've been working on this for months! Student of the month! That's a pretty nice honor, don't you think?"

Tim didn't hear what Missy whispered.

"Tracey? She doesn't mean anything to me. You know that, don't you?"

"Then where were you when I called last night? You said you needed help with chemistry. You weren't home at seven and you weren't home at eleven."

"Yeah? Well, I was at practice. You know we have to stay late sometimes."

"I'll bet you do. But not on a school night. I'm tired of your excuses, and I'm sick of being humiliated. I've had it with you and that group of kids you've been hanging with. You may fool everyone else, but you don't fool me. If your parents knew, they'd—"

"Yeah? And you'd tell them, I suppose." John was mad. Roughly he grabbed her. Then, as if remembering where he was, he removed his hands from her shoulders and directed her down the hall.

This time Missy stopped. Tim saw her look up as John's six-foot-three frame towered over her. *I wish I were that tall,* Tim thought.

"That's it!" he heard her say. "I don't want to see you or go out with you ever again. You won't two-time me! We're all washed up. Through!"

John turned beet red and swore at her. Then he turned on his heel and started down the hall. Suddenly he seemed unsteady on his feet. He reached out to catch the wall so that he wouldn't fall. *I wonder if he's high, or drunk,* Tim thought. *Maybe things aren't so good after all.*

Then his thoughts turned to Missy. *Boy, did I misjudge her. I wonder if she really means it. I hope she doesn't see me. I don't want to embarrass her. Hmm, today could be my lucky day. I'd sure like to date her.*

The rest of the day seemed to drag on forever. When the two o'clock bell finally rang, Tim hurried to his locker and then rushed outside. Missy was boarding the bus alone. No one was there saying good-bye to her. *She's a survivor,* Tim thought. *No one can take her pride away from her. Maybe I'll call her tonight to see* if *she'll help me with chemistry.*

When he was leaving school, snow was just beginning to fall, and there was a new chill in the air. He headed for the gas station where he worked, four blocks away. The clock above the door reminded him that in the future, he'd need to hurry to get to work on time. But the walk in the snow was beautiful, especially since he had someone on his mind. The job was boring, though, and he was glad when five-thirty came and it was time to go.

As he walked the mile to his house, the snow continued to fall gently. In the dark, the road was slippery and treacherous underfoot. Tim pulled his ski hat down over his ears and tugged the zipper of his parka up as far as it would go. Buffered against the cold, he walked as fast as he dared, and he was relieved when he saw his porch light gleaming in the distance.

At home he burst through the front door and headed straight into the den where his mother already had a fire blazing. He fell into his father's recliner and removed his boots. The six o'clock news was on, and he was aware of the announcer's warning of icy roads and traffic snarls downtown. Even now, there were reports of skidding accidents and people stranded because of the weather. Tim hoped his father was okay. Minutes later he was immensely relieved to hear the crunch of tires in the driveway and then the door opening.

After supper, Tim went into the den to study, but he couldn't concentrate. Shakespeare was just too hard to read. *I wish I liked basketball. If I were "number one," maybe some of my teachers would be willing to overlook my uninspired academic performance. I wouldn't mind being sought after by girls and colleagues. I'm too much of a dreamer, I guess. Why do I have to read this stuff anyway? Maybe I'll call Missy. Maybe she'll help me.* He imagined her, smiling at him, as he started for the telephone.

But he was sidetracked. The anchorman for Channel 9 news had just interrupted the program with an emergency bulletin. As Tim listened he became increasingly alarmed. There had been a serious accident on Route 32, north of Worthington. Three cars and a semi were involved. One car had skidded out of control into the lane of the oncoming truck. The truck had hit the car, pushing it back into its original lane, where it collided with two others and then skidded on black ice, hit the shoulder, and turned over.

A picture of the accident flashed across the screen. It made Tim feel sick. The car, or what remained of it, was a red Porsche, the top completely crushed in.

"Four young people are in critical condition," the commentator continued. Tim couldn't listen anymore. He turned off the television and went into the kitchen. His mother and father stopped talking when they saw his face. He told them what he had seen. "Should I call her?" he asked.

"Who?"

"Missy. John's girlfriend."

"No. I'd wait until you know more," his father said.

His mother agreed. "There's always a chance it wasn't the same car," she added.

In his heart, Tim knew the truth. He remembered his walk home on the black ice masked by the whiteness of the new snow. Suddenly he felt overwhelmed by guilt. *I wished for this*, he thought. *I must really have hated that kid, and that's not fair. I would never have wished this on him. Poor Missy. She'll blame herself for this.*

By nine o'clock Tim's fears were confirmed. He dialed Missy's number, but there was no answer. At eleven he tried again. There was still no answer. Finally, he went up to bed, physically and emotionally exhausted. After a while, he slipped into a troubled sleep.

In his dream, he was standing alone in the middle of a field that stretched on through the darkness. The land was flat, with snow-covered stubble, standing like knives against the moonlight. The corn seemed scorched and black under the snow patches, and the desolation was frightening. A house with a small light stood off in the distance. Tim was irresistibly drawn toward it, and he began walking. The wind chilled him to the bone, and he lost track of time and distance.

When he got there, he found the door ajar, so he went in. He called out, but there was no answer. As he looked around the room, the truth came to him. On the table was a collection of drug paraphernalia, things he'd learned about in health class. He had no idea how recently they'd been used. He looked in the refrigerator. There he saw bottles of liquor.

Then he heard the sound of crying. At first, it was a low moaning sound, but as the wind picked u, it grew louder and louder.

Suddenly the door burst open. The scene before him was horrible. Tim cowered in his chair as the screaming bodies raced across the threshold. Tracey appeared, moving like a shadow. She was disfigured and covered in blood. The others that followed were injured beyond recognition. Tim heard the crackling of flames. He looked beyond them all and saw the car.

He covered his eyes. When he opened them, he was outside the house. It was ablaze, and the victims inside were screaming.

* * *

He awoke, grateful to find himself in his own bed. A faint light glimmered in the eastern sky. Remnants of darkness lurked in the corners of his room and shadows darted across his mirror. He was sweating profusely. "I don't ever want to know the whole story," he said aloud. "Thank God I'm alive." He pulled the covers back over his head and tried to sleep, but it was pointless. All he could think about was Missy and what had happened to the others. He decided to get up and go to school for Missy's sake.

Even for Tuesday, the halls were very quiet. Students sat in near silence, subdued and without spirit. A few were crying. The teachers showed the strain of their tragedy.

Missy wasn't in school. Tim wasn't surprised that she needed to be away from Worthington High. They would all have to face up to their feelings about what had happened, and for some, this would mean turning to friends for support. But Missy wasn't like that.

The principal's voice over the intercom was an intrusion. As he began talking about yesterday's tragedy and about grief, Tim heard the names: "John Mathias, Tracey Houle, Bob Henson, and Janet Snow," all of them popular kids. *Worthington's finest*, Tim thought cynically. He knew why they had died. His dream had only reaffirmed what he already suspected. By evening, the community would know about the poison in their blood. The town would reel with denial—"substance abuse doesn't happen in a town like Worthington"—but then the families would go on living and maybe even face the realities of drug abuse.

The voice on the intercom droned on. *Adults are so far away from us*, Tim thought.

At the end of the week, Tim went to the funeral home after school. He signed the book and shook hands with the parents of the four kids who'd been alive four days before. The lines were long, with people of all ages attending in homage to the victims of the town's tragedy.

Finally Tim found Missy, sitting in a corner, opposite the closed caskets. He went to her. They didn't talk, but he sat with his arm around her shoulders for a long time. She looked up at him, weeping, and then turned away. Tim's heart was hurting. He stayed with her for as long as he could stand it.

The next morning he attended the funeral with hundreds of other people. Yet he felt very much alone. *It's like a national tragedy*, he thought. *These people represent all the things we stand for—achievement in school, potential for the future, pride in our town, and success in life. And it was all torn away in an instant.*

Tim mourned with the others. He heard the minister conclude his talk with a quote from a poem he'd heard in English class. It was about an athlete who had died when he was still young and famous. *The difference is ironic*, Tim thought. Crowned in laurel, the athlete was carried through the streets like John was carried through the halls. But a question about John loomed in Tim's mind. *Why had this incredibly successful athlete taken drugs?*

Maybe life isn't that simple, Tim thought. *I admit I was jealous of John, but we build a guy up and forget what it takes to live life at the top. We support what he does and forget who he is. Maybe the pressure of staying on top was too much, and drugs were his way out. And now the drugs have killed him. Maybe I've been too tough on him.*

His thoughts shifted to himself. *It isn't just what you do in life that counts. It's what you stand for and how you achieve your goals. Being average is okay, unless you aren't giving your best effort. And criticizing a top achiever isn't fair. What you have a right to criticize is a value system and whether a person follows that system. If a person is a two-timer, you can take him to task for that; but if he's an addict, he needs help. That's where parents, schools, and peers all let each other down.*

For me, I need to accept what I am and be true to myself. Excuses are unacceptable.

On Monday morning Missy was at her locker. Tim took her books and put his arm around her shoulder. "Do you want to talk about it?"

"Well, maybe."

"After school?"

She nodded.

"I'll meet you by the front steps," Tim said.

Mary's

The Tent

I was walking in the west field, swishing through the tall, wet grass, to my favorite spot. I just wanted to get under the large oak tree that overlooked Clearwater Brook. On that little rise, there was always enough breeze to cool off. I sat down on the rock ledge, leaned against my favorite tree, and opened my lunch bag. The food inside was nothing special—just a peanut butter and jelly sandwich and a banana—but it was the comfort food I needed. The simple lunch and the cool water in my canteen were better than any feast.

Afterward, I stretched out on my back and relaxed. The patches of sky that showed through the branches were incredibly blue, and, except for the occasional clacking of the grasshoppers, all was quiet and very peaceful.

But that was ten years ago. I'm eighteen now, and the memory of that particular field will always be with me.

I don't know why my Aunt Liz sent me to a summer farm camp. Maybe she was tired of having an eight-year-old around. Maybe I just wasn't worthy of her attention. Maybe she didn't like my name, but what's wrong with a name like Mary? Maybe my mother had gotten sicker from the divorce, and I would never be able to go home again. I just couldn't understand any of it. So I had run off to the barn and spent most of the day tunneling into the hay, trying to escape from being unhappy. When I finally emerged from my tunnel and climbed up to the loft, it was too hot to breathe. Outside I could see the thunderheads building. Even if I had to face the taunts of the other girls, I knew it was time to get back to the farmhouse for supper.

But I never made it. Suddenly, it was pouring and the torrents forced me into my new sleeping quarters, a little tent, located a good distance from the house. I'd stay there for the night and forget supper. Now the darkness settled in, strangely comforting, considering the events that had forced me into this little prison in the glade.

Stiff stalks of grass and low-growing branches grazed the sides of the tent as the wind blew wildly, and brilliant flashes of lightening shown through the thick canvas roof. As the thunder's sonic boom sent me, cringing, further down inside the rough flannel lining of my sleeping bag, I squeezed my eyelids shut tight. I found my flashlight and clicked it on, but it was useless. Its reflector barely had a chance to catch the cold metal zipper and drab olive green of my surroundings before the bulb flickered and went out, and the pale pathway of light that had connected me to the reality of my surroundings disappeared forever.

I was utterly alone in my tight, triangular web of retreat. For the moment I felt warm and comfortable and secure, enclosed by darkness and confined space. Soon, I drifted, weightless and without feeling, into a world without definition.

Who knows how much time passed or how long I slept. All I know is that when I awoke, there was such a dank, unpleasant odor of rain on mildewed canvas that I could hardly breathe. Suddenly my mouth was dry with fear. My muscles tensed, and my heart started racing. I tried to take deep breaths, but my throat wouldn't cooperate. The overwhelming humidity and odor of this place was stifling.

The steady *drip, drip, drip* of rain droplets through the leaky roof chilled the back of my neck just along the hairline. The musty tarpaulin, which was supposed to have protected me, had slipped all the way down to my waist.

A chill of disgust raced through me. As my hair, damp and matted, clung to the edges of my face and ears, I shook involuntarily. I curled up, understanding now that the unpleasantness of these sensations paralleled being alone. Feeling completely inadequate at any task, I retreated further into the dry, still-warm lower recesses of my sleeping bag.

The wind surged again. Like circus whips, the door flaps snapped open, taunting me to get up and secure the straps. In complete darkness I pushed back the tarpaulin and the sleeping bag, preserving what dryness I could before I got up. At first my bare feet jerked back from the cold rubberized floor, but then I stumbled toward the wildly flapping canvas. I snatched the cloth doors from the wind's angry grasp and, struggling, tied them down. At once I was fierce with energy as I groped for the entrance back to my nest.

Suddenly, I felt frozen in time, assaulted by those memories again. My mother's worried pale face and her thin body loomed before my eyes. She was so frail, and I hadn't even seen it. Here I was now, lonely and resentful and scared, because she had deserted me, and I couldn't run to her for help. She couldn't know I was trying to understand why she had abandoned me. And it wasn't only that. I didn't have any friends either. Just bullies that I had been forced to share a tent with. And I ran away from them because I couldn't stand being laughed at and pushed around. Besides, they were older and they'd been to this camp before. They weren't here because they didn't have any other place to go. They liked this place.

I could still hear them teasing.

"Come on, Mary. It's morning. Time to get up and empty the pot. Hurry up! It smells in here. Pinch her! Roll her around! Pull her out of bed! That'll wake her up!"

And, of course, it did.

The scene rolled over me again, wrapping around me like a giant mist. Wet and crying, my feelings spilled out into the stormy night. "I hate you! I hate you! I hate you!" I yelled out angry words at the girls far across the fields, who had bullied me four mornings in a row to empty that horrid, ammonia-smelling pot. Then I had run from them, not knowing how to make them take their turns. As the youngest, how was I to fight back and deal with these bullies?

My outburst ceased. As I settled back into my nest, my heart stopped pounding, and my clenched fists relaxed. I felt better. Once again the warmth lulled me into fantasies—this time, of hot chocolate with lots of whipped cream and warm buttered cinnamon rolls. My mouth was watering. I was so empty and so hungry.

Mary M. Nyman

And then, as I was lying there, wanting so desperately to escape this prison of my own making, I was suddenly aware of a sound beyond the wind. It was unrelated— almost imperceptible, but soft and reassuring. I felt the small pressure of one—two, and—then four little feet on top of the tarpaulin. A low, comforting purr was coming from the muff of silky, warm fur as the kitten snuggled her way into my damp sleeping bag. I may have been lonely and lost, but I was no longer alone. In that endless night, we became sister spirits, fixed in time and mutually protected against the storm.

Looking back on that night, I now understand what I have always felt, and that is that comfort can come from small, unexpected events that can change our lives forever. And when they do, they help us believe that forces greater than we will ever know can save us from the storms we experience within.

Janet's

Daydreaming

The sun shone bright and hot, and the Michigan sky was cornflower blue. When their station wagon rounded the crest of the hill, Janet gasped in anticipation as she looked down across the field and the railroad tracks at the cottages nestled along the shore. *Yes,* she thought, *the lake was like a dream*—still one of the most beautiful lakes she had ever seen. It called her with its crystal clear water in three shades of turquoise blue.

"Oh, Mom," she exclaimed, "let's hurry. I can't wait to jump in!"

She had spent every summer here since she could remember. In fact, she had celebrated every birthday in the dining room overlooking the lake. She felt warm and happy just remembering it. And soon she would celebrate this most important birthday, her sixteenth, with all its advantages and privileges.

She imagined herself in front of the window overhung by pines that whispered in the wind. The evening sun threw its rippling torch across the lake, creating a spectacular effect—it was called Torch Lake for this reason. She imagined her mother bringing in a large cake with lemon icing flowers as her friends rushed in, shouting "Happy Birthday!" Being reunited each summer with Jennifer next door was something she always looked forward to. Then she thought about Gram's special sixteenth birthday check. And, finally, she would see it—a large, shiny Camaro in the driveway. She watched herself hopping behind the wheel, waving good-bye, and zooming away in a cloud of dust. She spun around the curve and screeched to a halt at the railroad crossing. It was just in time, too, as the Pere Marquette rumbled by on its way to the northern woods. She cruised up the highway, passing her cousin's house, the Wild Wind Amusement Park and the Blue Parrot Night Club. "Whoops! I'm going too fast." She slowed down but not before the blue lights were visible in her rearview mirror. She instinctively slammed on her brakes—*Exactly what I'm not supposed to do*, she remembered too late.

Oh, there I go, daydreaming again. As they pulled into the yard behind the cottage, she wondered if she had spoken aloud because of the way her mother was looking at her. Her mother always knew when she was off in her own world, and Janet sensed she understood her well enough not to interfere. *Thank goodness for mothers like mine*, she thought.

The station wagon jolted to a halt, and everyone—Janet, her mother, her twelve-year-old brother, the two dogs, and Seedy, the cat—tumbled out of the car. Janet and Jason knew enough to carry everything in without being asked. The cooler was automatically deposited in the kitchen, and clothes, shoes, trash, and the rest of the stuff from their eight-hundred-mile trip found its way into bedrooms, wastebaskets, and the dirty clothes hamper. Janet rushed upstairs to her bedroom under the eaves. She immediately felt at ease there, where the wind and rain could always comfort her and lull her to sleep.

Then they all went for a dip. The swim was a yearly ritual, meant to cleanse the body and spirit of the responsibilities of home and their accustomed daily routines. After this, the summer vacation would truly begin.

Two perfect days went by, and everyone felt renewed. Janet liked not having to babysit for her neighbor's bratty four-year-old. And not having to work whenever they called her at the Kozy Ice Cream Parlor was nice, too. She liked not having to arrange for rides when it was raining or call her mother to come get her at midnight. And she liked not having to do any more required summer reading. It was such a relief to be here for vacation, immersed in her own very special world.

Her birthday came and went. No gang of friends greeted her, but her mother, brother, and Jennifer, her friend from next door, were there to sing "Happy Birthday," while a brilliant orange sun set across the lake. The cake's lemon-flavored icing was delicious, and a promise of the driver's ed course and a chance for her license came to her in writing from her mother. Especially important was her grandmother's gift. Her check for twenty thousand dollars had arrived, registered mail, that morning. *Red Camaro, here I come!*

Several days later, Janet awoke, feeling that something was terribly wrong. It was while she was taking an early morning swim that her fears were confirmed. Her mother called her to come in, with an urgency in her voice that made Janet hurry. She jumped up on the dock, dried her feet, and ran up the stone steps to the house.

She couldn't believe her mother's pale, shaky appearance. "Janet," she said, hesitantly, "it's your grandmother."

An icy fear gripped Janet. *What could have happened?* When they left home, Gram had been doing so much better after the fall that had left her with a broken hip six weeks before. She had even started using her walker again. And she had a friend staying with her to help. At eighty-one, she was in good spirits and worry-free and ready to see her family head off to Michigan for the rest of the summer. As it was, their usual vacation had been delayed several weeks because of her injury. She'd said, "School will be starting before you know it, and you all need to spend some time at the lake. I'm in good hands here, so you don't need to worry."

Typical of Gram, Janet thought, *always putting other people first.* She had felt pangs of guilt about leaving her grandmother, first in the rehabilitation center and then at home, even though the care she was receiving was excellent, and her mother had felt that it was safe to leave.

"Mom," she said, "what happened?"

Her mother was crying now. "Oh, Janet, Gram has developed pneumonia. The doctors said she became ill very suddenly. They don't know what to tell us except that the prognosis is not good. They're very concerned."

I don't want to leave, Janet thought. *Why does this have to happen now?* Her feelings for Gram and her gram's generosity complicated the situation even more. It had only been right to give up time at the lake to stay near her grandmother. But if she felt resentful about those daily visits to the rehab center, she also felt guilty now about not being there. Gram was so generous and so caring and was always looking out for them. What if she died before they got home?

She knew they would have to leave immediately. Within an hour they were ready to make the long trip home again. As they piled into the station wagon, Jason seemed unusually quiet—not grumbly and argumentative like he usually was.

They arrived in Johnsonville the next afternoon. A depressing rain was falling, turning everything gray and cold. The hospital where Gram had been moved was terribly quiet, and it smelled of alcohol and disinfectant. *Intensive care. That's where Gram is.* Janet knew before her mother told her.

They went in while Jason waited in the car with the animals. They took the elevator to the second floor and stopped at the nurses' station. Then they tiptoed into the darkened room where Gram lay, frail and small beneath a stark-white sheet. She was hooked up to tubes and monitors and machines that made strange little beeping noises. The worst thing was Gram's face. Even in the dim light, she was chalk white. Janet wondered whether she was still alive.

I'm not ready for this. I don't want to see her die. I want her to wake up and talk to me and smile like she always does. What's wrong with this hospital? What have they done to her?

Janet was aware that her mother had stepped out of the room. She was talking quietly to the nurses under the glare of the desk light. Suddenly Janet knew the truth. *Gram is dying. She isn't ever going to talk to us again. She doesn't even know we are here. I can't even thank her for my present or tell her how much I love her. Please, God, let her know we are here.*

There was no response, and Janet knew she would have to get away from the sight in front of her. *Why*, she wondered, *did we have to come back to this? I want to remember my grandmother like she was, smiling and talking—not like this, hooked up to all these machines. This isn't my grandmother. It's a corpse, with electrical impulses forcing life into it.*

"Mom," she cried out, "make them take those things out of her." Janet backed out of the room and ran into the waiting room to cry. A few minutes later, her mother came in and sat down beside her. Without saying a word, she put her arms around Janet and pulled her close. Gram was gone.

***

After the funeral three days later, everyone felt a terrible emptiness. The rain continued, almost, it seemed, as a reflection of the sadness everyone was feeling. *Why did Gram have to die before her time?* Janet pondered. *But then, is there ever any appropriate time for someone you love to leave you?*

Her mother drove all that night while Janet and her brother slept. By the next evening they were back at the cottage.

The memory of Gram's frail and helpless body hooked up to all those machines and the hollowness Janet was feeling would stay with her for a long time. Not being able to say good-bye was very painful, but it was easier to be here than at home. Somehow it was better to look out at the lake and think about Gram's death. The serenity and beauty of this place helped her achieve some balance between her thoughts and her feelings, and this experience gave her some perspective.

The hardest thing to deal with, Janet thought, *is that someone can slip away from you when you least expect it. You've been lost in your daydreams, and you're so caught up in trying to grow up that you keep waiting to move from one step to another. You could hardly wait to be sixteen, to attain some status in your school, and to get a chance to drive. But, as time passes and you achieve these things, you're always losing something else you may not even be aware of. It's like wishing your own life away.*

Janet knew she could not have prevented Gram's dying. But now she knew she must consider the decisions she would make in her own life. She wasn't daydreaming this time. Although Gram's gift was unrestricted, there would be no red Camaro. Gram's check would be banked for college. Janet decided that, from that point on, her academic performance would be excellent, so she could get into a college and prove herself worthy of her grandmother's wishes. She knew she could make the right decisions, too. Gram had set a very strong example for her to follow.

Daydreams were lovely, but she was sixteen now, and it was time to start facing what life was all about.

Janet smiled to herself. It was nighttime again, and she heard the gentle rain on the roof and the wind in the trees. She knew her grandmother would approve of her decisions, and she knew she would sleep with her grandmother's presence in her heart.

Kenny's

Amos Goes to Smiling Hill Farm

Well, I'm Kenny, and I'm fourteen. I live with my mom in a big old house overlooking the Atlantic Ocean. We're at the end of a long dirt road that cuts through a forest of pine and oak trees that never seems to end, especially when you're walking home from the bus stop.

It's a perfect place for all the wild animals that live around us. In the back orchard we have deer that eat our apples and rabbits that keep trying to get into the garden. In front of our house we see hawks, gulls, ospreys, and lots of other water birds. There are too many to identify. We're like a kind of wilderness zoo. We've got foxes, skunks, opossums and, of course, my problem—Amos.

I guess I should call this *The Trouble with Amos* because he's really what this story is all about. If you know anything about raccoons, you know they can be a lot of fun because they're so curious. But they're a lot of trouble, too, because they are so mischievous. The problem starts when you have to make a decision about what to do with them. But I'm getting ahead of myself.

It all started the day Amos got into our neighbor's house. He just walked in, friendly and playful, as usual. Actually, that's not the whole truth. What he really did was break and enter, so to speak. The door happened to be open, but the screen was closed, so he just stood up on his hind legs and churred to come in like he always does. When nobody came to let him in, he grabbed the screen with his little hands and ripped it open with his teeth. At least that's what I heard.

By the time I arrived, there was mass confusion. I was met by Amos, who was tearing around the living room like a creature possessed by the devil. He was having a great time knocking over the plants and knickknacks and then diving for the newspapers and magazines. He was into everything.

Everyone was yelling and screaming, and next thing I knew, our neighbor was chasing him around with a broom. At that point Amos headed for the dining room. Up on a chair he went. He leaped to the table, slid all the way across, and took the lace cloth, glasses, and silverware with him. He dove for the floor, and everything landed in a messy pile on top of him.

As you can imagine, I was mortified. But Amos was just being mischievous. He started after one of the guests, nipping at his heels the way he usually does when he wants to play rough. By then everyone was frantic. Nobody could understand that Amos loved to chase feet and bite them, gently of course, without breaking the skin. It was all a game to him.

Finally someone kicked my little friend out the door and then hit him over the head with a stick, knocking him off the deck into the bushes below. While I was trying to decide how to handle the situation, I saw him picking up his bruised little body and eyeing everyone resentfully. He turned his back on all of us and limped off into the woods.

I didn't know what to say except that I was dreadfully sorry and that my big brother would fix the screen. In the meantime my mother came over. She tried to calm everyone down, but it was hard to do because our friends weren't used to dealing with wild animals. They love the wilderness, but it's hard for them to accept the fact that the animals that live around here need their space, too. And Amos had done a lot of damage. Of course my mother offered to replace all of the broken dishes.

If you live in the wilderness, you have to live among the animals. If your raccoon gets into the house, it isn't any worse than the deer and wild coons getting into the garden. At least Amos will follow you outside if you give him a peanut butter sandwich. It's all in how you handle and understand him.

You have to be philosophical about it. My mother and I disagree, however. She was pretty upset about the whole business, mainly because she'd gotten too attached to Amos and didn't want to admit it. She was afraid that if he bothered anyone else, it would be reported or, worse yet, he'd get shot, or someone would take us to court for having a wild animal as a pet. My mother's never been to court in her life.

I don't think anything like that will happen, but you never know. Fear makes people do all sorts of things you wouldn't expect, and having wild animals isn't a usual thing to do.

Well, after this embarrassing incident, my mother went away on her annual trip south. It was kind of nice having her gone. I didn't have to do the dishes or take out the trash for a week. But I sure missed Amos, and I had a pretty big job on my hands the day before Mom was due back. I had to get rid of all those big black ants in the garbage. They were marching all over the kitchen, too. If Amos had been there, he sure could have helped. He would have eaten the whole army in two minutes.

When my mother finally returned, Amos still hadn't come back. She figured he'd gone for good. On one hand she said she was glad he'd gone. But, on the other hand, she missed his little churring greetings and his games.

Well, things were pretty quiet in our house for another week. Then our cousins came to visit. It was a really hot night until ten o'clock, when a slight breeze came up. My mother was out feeding our dogs. When she came in, she had that faraway look in her eyes. I knew something was up.

"I'm sure Amos is out there."

"Aw, Mom, you're just imagining things," I told her.

"No. I heard a noise in the woods. It was that kind of low growl that only a coon can make."

You're just wishing, I thought, but I didn't say it. I didn't want to upset her.

But she kept it up. A little later she called me to come out again. It was too dark to see anything, and the wind was blowing through the oak trees, so it was hard to hear. "Don't you hear him panting?"

"Aw, Mom," I said.

"Listen. Can't you hear something?"

To be honest, I couldn't. Coons do tend to pant when they're excited or annoyed. Still, all I could hear was the wind in the trees.

35

Not to stretch this out, my mother proved her point. She went back into the house for a peanut butter sandwich, and, sure enough, Amos scrambled down the tree minutes later. With the sandwich, we bribed him to come into the house. My cousins really liked all the drama.

Now we were in a dilemma. We had Amos back, but it was still summer, and none of our neighbors had gone back to the city. So Amos had to be kept penned up in the back shed. This was all fine until he decided he wanted to be outside again. He'd already removed some of the panes of glass from the door connecting the house to the shed, and now he was working on removing the jalousies on the door that led outside to the patio. My brother nailed screen and boards over the inside door, so it looked like our house had been condemned.

Finally, Amos got outside again and went up his favorite tree, forcing us to go through the whole business of bribing him to come down again. To make matters worse, my mother calculated he'd done at least five hundred dollars' worth of damage to the two doors. This was in addition to taking up thirty-four tiles on our front porch, where he had lived the winter before.

The time had come. We had to make a decision. The most logical place for Amos to go was a game farm, and we knew of one that was two hundred miles away in Maine. It took two days to make the arrangements.

At five thirty on Saturday morning, we loaded Amos, our German shepherd, a cat carrier, and a cooler stocked with grapes, peanuts, water, and dog food into our car. We had a four-hour trip ahead of us.

Amos spent most of the trip on my shoulder, sleeping. Then he wrestled with the dog for a while. He didn't make any mistakes to speak of, since he's litter box trained. And only once did he give my mom a scare, when he crawled onto her lap and started honking the horn. You can imagine the looks of shock on the faces of other drivers when they passed us and glanced in our direction. It's a wonder we didn't get stopped by the police.

Four hours later we drove through the gates of the game farm. Amos was curious. He sniffed the pine-scented Maine air and then shook himself vigorously. We found the man who was to introduce Amos to his new home. He really cared for animals, and he hit it off with Amos immediately. That made me feel better.

Amos knew something was up, but he cooperated and went right in the old screened-in pheasant coop that housed new arrivals. There was another young coon there, and the two of them immediately became friends. As it turned out, this little coon was there because it was blind, and it would never be allowed to leave the game farm.

I guess I should explain why this game farm exists. Its main goal is to take in wild animals, rehabilitate them to live on their own, and then return them to the wilderness. Animals that come here are orphaned, injured, or dependent on people for their survival. I guess Amos fell into the last category, although he spent a lot of time on his own in the woods before he came back to us. He could take care of himself.

Mom was sad. She didn't want to say good-bye any more than I did. "But," she remarked, "if we had let him go at home and he got hurt or disappeared for good, we would have had a hard time dealing with that one." Here, at least, we would have to make a clean break with our favorite pet.

We said good-bye, but this turned out not to be the end of the story. Amos was to spend the winter at the game farm because it was getting too late in the year to let him go. He would be safe and cozy, and we could even visit him.

A month passed, and we decided to pay a visit, but Amos wasn't there. We learned that he and his little friend had been transferred, and he would not be returned to the wilderness after all. Instead, we could visit him at his new home, Smiling Hill Farm, in Westbrook, Maine.

After driving another sixty miles, we found him in his new surroundings. His enclosure was as large as my bedroom and filled with pine branches. There was also a large hollow tree to sleep in and protect him from the cold.

You should go visit him sometime. Smiling Hill Farm is a great place, with all sorts of animals housed as carefully as possible to simulate their natural habitats. I guess I should feel happy that Amos has such a nice place to live.

Last night, though, when I got home, I had a really weird dream. I had kidnapped Amos from the game farm. With him wrapped snugly in my jacket, I made my getaway—except on my way out, the gate crashed shut, and I almost didn't make it. A huge sign loomed in front of me. I hadn't paid any attention to it when we went there, but now it became a giant reminder of the Amos story. In very large letters it read, "Wild animals do not make good pets."

I don't have to tell you that I woke up with some pretty mixed emotions. My mother would say she agrees with what the sign says, but I wonder if she really believes that. It is comforting to know that Amos is well cared for, though. Stories like this, I'm told, sometimes have unhappy endings.

Anne's

A Shaft of Sudden Light

It was a rainy day in December. Ara's father had just died, and Anne didn't want to go to the funeral.

Why should I have to go? she thought. *I hate funerals. They are just rituals anyway, just a way to comfort the living and reassure them that their loved one has gone to a better place.* Besides, she hadn't been friends with Ara since that horrid day in September.

What happened to us? Anne wondered. *We used to be so close.* Remembering sent her thoughts spiraling back to when the two of them had ridden their new bikes fast as the wind, pretending they were riding white stallions into the sunset. Those were such happy, carefree times. Then Anne's father had died in August, and Ara had been right there, comforting her at the funeral.

Losing her father had been traumatic enough, but then, in November, Anne's grandmother had died, too, leaving Anne in an emotional void. This recent memory was still so painful that she cried whenever she thought about it. She had always been able to talk to Gram when she was hurting or needed advice. But now she felt alone, and her feelings of anxiety and depression—not to mention her ambivalence toward Ara—were threatening to overwhelm her.

Even her counselor couldn't help her retrieve the remnants of light that usually surrounded her and were the basis for the drama in her paintings. Depression had its very dark side, and she met it going around corners, without warning and without preparation. The day gremlins, as Anne called them, resurfaced after nightmares that left

39

her extraordinarily weak and tearful. Always there was anxiety and those imaginary accidents—cars colliding, getting caught in mountain avalanches and mudslides, and dropping off the edge of the world. She knew these fears were irrational, yet she still couldn't keep them from invading her thoughts, and no one understood that. She was floundering in a life that sometimes seemed meaningless to her, and she just wanted to withdraw from it all.

But none of that really mattered now that Ara's father had died. What mattered most was addressing her anger and resentment. She knew that, but why couldn't her mother understand why she didn't want to attend the funeral?

She also knew the real reason for her feelings. She was hurt, really, and it was a matter of pride. It was always easier to put the blame somewhere else because she and Ara hadn't talked for several months. Yet, for nine years, they had been best friends. Their estrangement began in September, on Anne's first day back in her hometown high school. Because of her mother's financial situation, she had not been able to return to Southfield, the private school where she had spent her junior year.

So there she was, in a public school, as a senior who had been away from the people she thought were her friends. However, lots of things can happen when you are away. Cliques can form and impressions really count. Her first day there turned out to be a nightmare.

Anne had assumed that things would be the same. She would reconnect with Ara and the others, and they would go to class and then lunch, as usual.

But it didn't happen that way. Instead, Ara gave her the ultimate brush-off. She didn't even welcome her back or ask how she was doing. She was too busy impressing the group, maybe, or Mr. Whatever-His-Name-Was, the handsome new guy on the block. *Who knows and who cares*, Anne had thought, because at lunch it was even worse. There was no place for her to sit.

She relived that moment of shame and loneliness. Her face flushed just thinking about how betrayed she had felt, standing alone in the middle of the cafeteria. *Ara, you are so hateful*, she'd thought to herself, *and I hate you, too!* After that, they didn't talk to each other, and their estrangement grew larger than life.

Now Ara's father had passed away after suffering a massive heart attack, and Anne remembered how Ara had been there for her when her father had died. Ara and her mother had sat across the aisle from Anne's family in the dark church. The memory was sudden and vivid, but the message was unmistakable. She knew she must go to the funeral.

***

In church, Anne was completely unprepared for the rush of feeling she experienced when the casket was wheeled in, and Ara began shaking uncontrollably across the aisle. To make matters worse, at that moment a shaft of light broke through the stained glass window and touched Ara, creating an almost halolike effect. *An accusing symbol*, Anne thought. Suddenly, she experienced such an enormous sense of loss, grief, and guilt. The power of losing a father, a grandmother, and a friend was overwhelming.

Ara turned her head. Anne saw her tears and felt her extreme distress as their eyes met. But Ara turned away quickly and didn't look at her again.

Suddenly everything came together for Anne. This brief and painful moment of communication was not only about death. It was about living. *Life is all about relationships, then, and these are governed by the inexplicable feeling that ultimately translates into love. That is what God is all about. Not rituals, really, but just that overwhelming feeling of understanding and responding to the heart.*

Like that shaft of sudden light, the windows of the soul were suddenly flung open, and Anne forgave her friend. Death was happening again, and Anne knew she could help Ara handle it. She also knew they would finally reconnect after the funeral.

Epilogue

After our meeting, we all left for home, going our separate ways. But we weren't really separate anymore. Writing and sharing our stories made us feel better understood, somehow more connected to one another, and more accepting of ourselves. In two months our writing club will meet again, and there will be more stories, more memories, and more sharing.

and my real friends accept and appreciate this. That is what happiness is all about. My life is a song that is only beginning.

"Hey, there goes Jenny. Wonder where her girlfriend is. Do you think they've got a hot date tonight? Wonder where they're going."

All I wanted to do was run and hide.

Then Sherri's attendance began to drop off. So did her grades. Here it was, almost the end of the school year, and she was a junior. Maintaining good grades was becoming even more crucial. But even with everything that was going on, nothing could have prepared me for what happened next. And learning about it at school didn't help either.

It was Friday, and I hadn't seen her since Thursday afternoon. We both needed to study for big tests, and we decided not to see each other or telephone that evening.

It was one of those snitches that clued me in. Her dad had a police scanner. The 911 call at six-thirty that morning had given the address and the situation. Sherri had taken a bunch of pills and was in Glenn Hospital. She was unconscious as far as anyone knew.

I freaked out. I was hysterical. One of my teachers shielded me and guided me into the nurse's office, and the nurse called my mother. After I was dismissed my mother drove me to the hospital. For once she didn't ask questions. I waited and waited outside the emergency room. I have no idea how much time passed.

Finally I was allowed to go in. She was coming to, and she was groggy, but everyone knew she would pull through.

Thank God Sherri survived. However, our relationship didn't, mostly because of the awful pressures we faced from the other kids. They continued to taunt and be mean, and I think they blamed me for everything. We felt like we were under constant surveillance.

Sherri's grades continued to suffer, and she never regained her position of acceptance in the school.

After her senior year she went on to college, but, from then on, everything between us was awkward. It was so sad. We still talked and saw each other occasionally, but we were on guard at every moment. At school I felt more alienated than ever.

For me, counseling was very helpful. My grades had really fallen off in high school, but I am now back on track academically. Presently I am taking art courses in college and planning for a future in teaching. And, most important, I finally feel good about myself. I am who I am,

"Well, so are you, silly." Her tone and her smile were so gentle . . .

"Me?" Her words made me feel shy and self-conscious. I looked down at the floor and stammered, "No, I'm not."

"Sure you are. You just have to believe in yourself." Sherri came to stand behind me, and she began to brush my hair. It seemed so innocent, and it felt so good. "You're prettier than you know," she murmured.

She ran her fingers through my hair, playing with it. Her touch was soft and warm. Then she continued brushing with long, slow, rhythmic strokes. I was lulled into complacency, and I closed my eyes and leaned back into her. The pleasure of being so close to her was unmistakable. I was in another world.

"I wish . . . I just wish . . . that I were as pretty as you. Then maybe you would—"

"Would what? Do what ...? Do this?"

She turned my face towards hers and kissed me. It was a gentle brush, her lips on mine. She was a good friend, and this seemed innocent enough, but suddenly my feelings were unleashed. The kisses deepened, and all I wanted to do was keep on kissing her. My heart was bursting. "Oh, Sherri—Is this for real?"

Suddenly, a high obscene squeal broke the spell. We jumped apart like we had been burned, but it was too late.

"Ooh la la!" sang out Nancy Griffiths. A snide giggle from her sidekick, Amber, followed. They were two of the biggest gossips in the school. They doubled over, laughing, as they ran out of the room. We stood there, staring at each other—silent, frozen, wide-eyed. We knew that within hours the incident would be all over school.

The next morning we found ourselves being treated like freaks. The repercussions were horrid. Within days, Sherri was no longer being looked up to, and even the teachers seemed to treat her differently, or so it seemed to me. And the snitches kept whispering and whispering, until I felt paranoid going into the girls' room alone. I was afraid I'd get beaten up. At home I was crying a lot.

Sherri had a lot more to lose than I did. I'd always kept a low profile at school. While I was a strong student, I didn't go out for extracurricular activities, and I certainly wasn't beauty queen material. But what do you do when you go down the hall and hear things like, wasn't overweight or clumsy like some of us were. She smiled a lot and laughed with everyone, and she cheered us up. She was friendly and sensitive and was a role model for all of us. And she was an excellent student who was respected by her peers and her teachers.

I just guessed it was part of my personality, that feeling of inadequacy, that drew me to her and her accomplishments. I imagined everyone would want to be like her. But when I looked at her and longed to be like her, there was something else I couldn't define. On top of that, I knew it wasn't normal to be attracted to a girl.

Maybe it was normal for me, but I was just unaware of it or could never admit it to myself. I had dreamed more than once about female teachers and even had crushes on them. One was my beautiful art teacher in the eighth grade, and another was my Sunday school teacher when I was twelve. I would dream that they were like mothers. They would hug and comfort me, and I felt so happy. *Was I just longing for a mother figure?* I wondered.

It could have all happened in the shower room. It is good that it didn't. What did happen was the sudden, unexplainable rush of feeling between us. I think Sherri was as confused as I was. She didn't know how to handle it either.

After school, when I got home and thought about things, I got scared. Then there was the phone call, and, before I knew it, she was at the front door. Was it fate that we lived around the corner from each other?

What happened afterward was a series of dizzying events that changed my life. Going outside that special day, when the sun came out and a glorious rainbow appeared, was harmless enough. And we just went for an ice cream. But seeing each other in school everyday after that was another matter.

It was something that happened in the locker room one afternoon that clinched the situation. Sherri was standing in front of the mirror, brushing her hair. I was fascinated. It was close to three o'clock, and the room was lit only by a faint glow from the small overhead window. But Sherri's hair caught every last hint of sunlight as it filtered down into the room. She was beautiful, and suddenly the world glimmered with possibilities.

"Oh, you're so pretty," I whispered.

Jennifer's

Jenny's Song

This story about my high school experience is personal. Maybe it's too personal, but I think I need to tell it because I'm not the only one I know who feels she doesn't fit in anywhere. Even now it is sometimes difficult to know where I belong.

It all began several years ago, when I was a freshman. It was spring, my favorite time of year, and the wisteria was blooming high up over the steps that led down to the driveway. The blooms were almost two feet long, and their fragrance was heavenly. I loved to look at their soft, inviting colors, and I studied them, wanting to try to capture their beauty in a painting in art class.

But I was afraid to go to school. It was the week after it happened, and everyone was whispering and talking about me. At least I felt like they were. When you walk down the hall and the people you thought were your friends avoid you, you know something isn't right. And when no one will sit with you at lunch, you just decide not to eat. So I began to feel more and more confused about the feelings I couldn't control.

I'm not sure when I sensed that I was different. I wanted to reach out to people and retreat from them at the same time. I wanted to be reassured that it was okay to feel the way I was feeling. I just couldn't come to grips with being different. But this all came to a head in May, and that is when these events took place.

I'd begun to notice Sherri in gym class. She was so beautiful that I couldn't take my eyes off her. It was like a fixation. She was tall and slender, with long, glossy black hair. She had bright blue eyes, and she

43